HAIR TODAY, GONE T

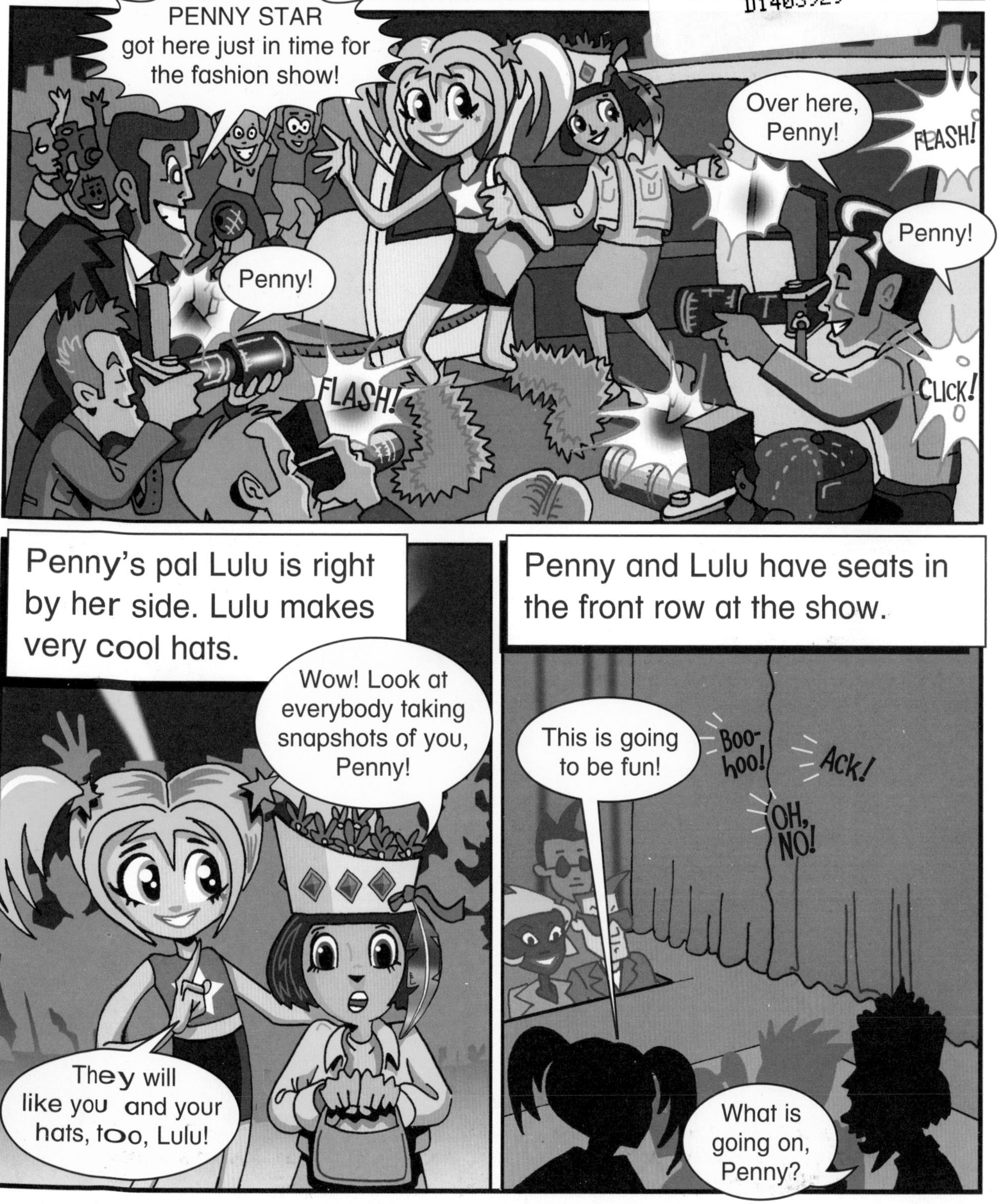
PENNY STAR got here just in time for the fashion show!
Over here, Penny!
FLASH!
Penny!
Penny!
FLASH!
CLICK!
Penny's pal Lulu is right by her side. Lulu makes very cool hats.
Wow! Look at everybody taking snapshots of you, Penny!
They will like you and your hats, too, Lulu!
Penny and Lulu have seats in the front row at the show.
This is going to be fun!
Boo-hoo!
ACK!
OH, NO!
What is going on, Penny?

The models come running out. What happened to their hair?

Oh, my poor hair!

My hair is gone!

Is my hair still there?

Eeek!

Then the models see Penny in the front row.

Penny Star! Help us, please!

Can you find the monster who did this to us?

The whole world knows that Penny Star is great at solving puzzles.

You bet I will help you.

Please stop with all the boo-hoos, and show me to your dressing rooms!

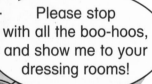

Here is my stuff. And look! This is me before my hair fell out!

SNIFF!

HAIR BE GOOD!

HAIR BE YELLOW!

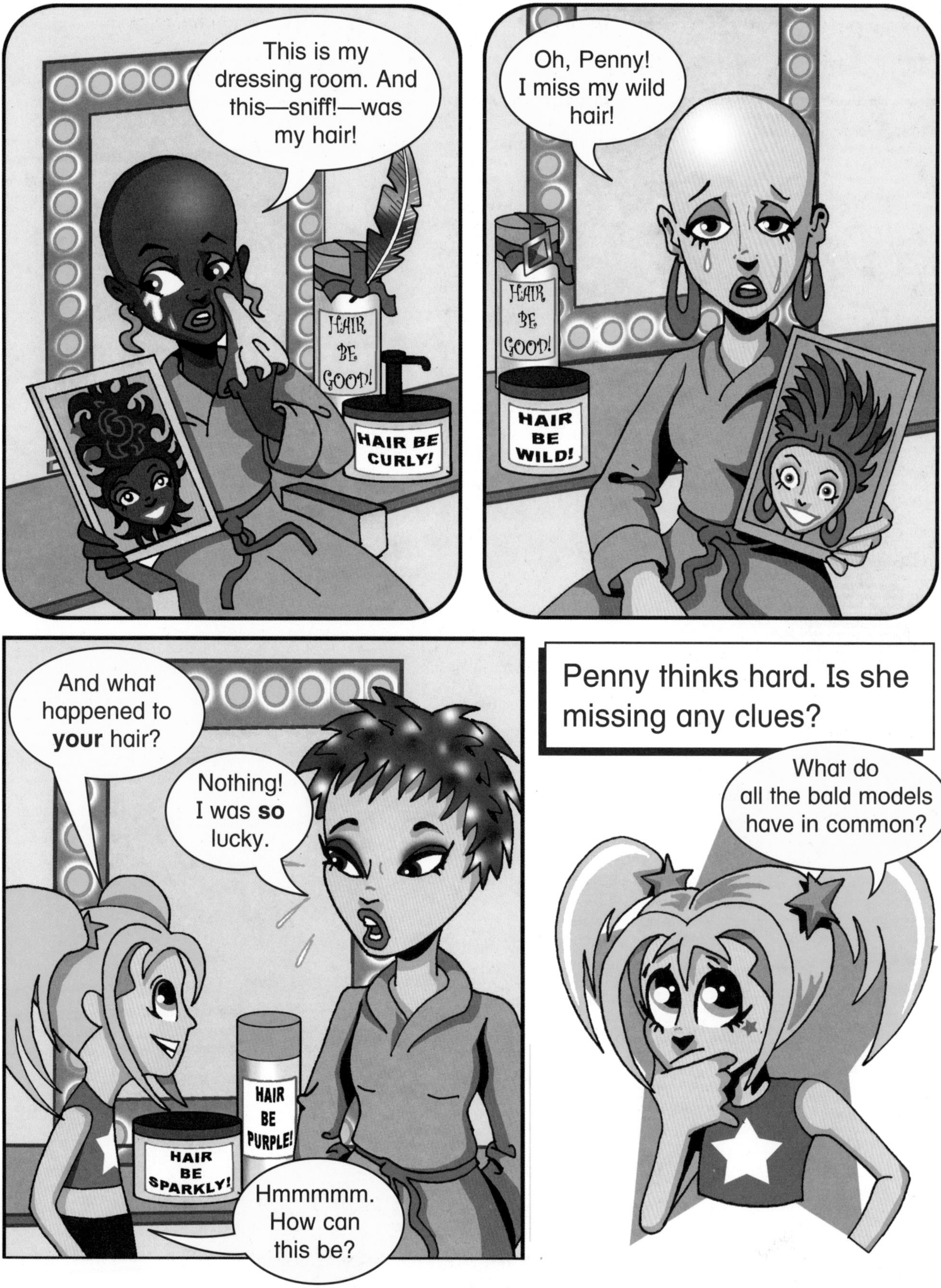
This is my dressing room. And this—sniff!—was my hair!
HAIR BE GOOD!
HAIR BE CURLY!
Oh, Penny! I miss my wild hair!
HAIR BE GOOD!
HAIR BE WILD!
And what happened to **your** hair?
Nothing! I was **so** lucky.
HAIR BE SPARKLY!
HAIR BE PURPLE!
Hmmmmm. How can this be?
Penny thinks hard. Is she missing any clues?
What do all the bald models have in common?

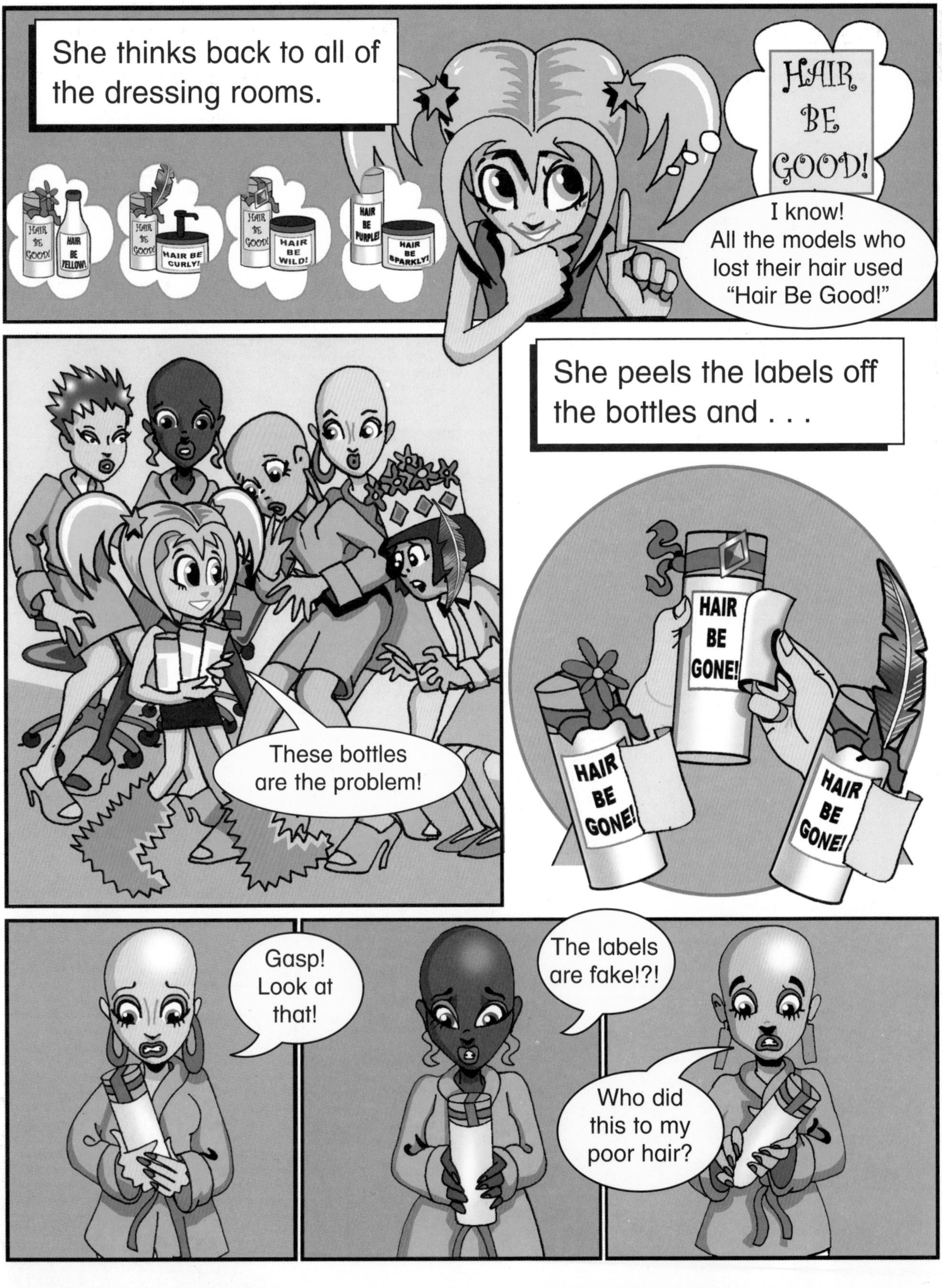
She thinks back to all of the dressing rooms.
HAIR BE GOOD!
HAIR BE YELLOW!
HAIR BE CURLY!
HAIR BE WILD!
HAIR BE PURPLE!
HAIR BE SPARKLY!
I know! All the models who lost their hair used "Hair Be Good!"
She peels the labels off the bottles and . . .
These bottles are the problem!
HAIR BE GONE!
HAIR BE GONE!
HAIR BE GONE!
Gasp! Look at that!
The labels are fake!?!
Who did this to my poor hair?

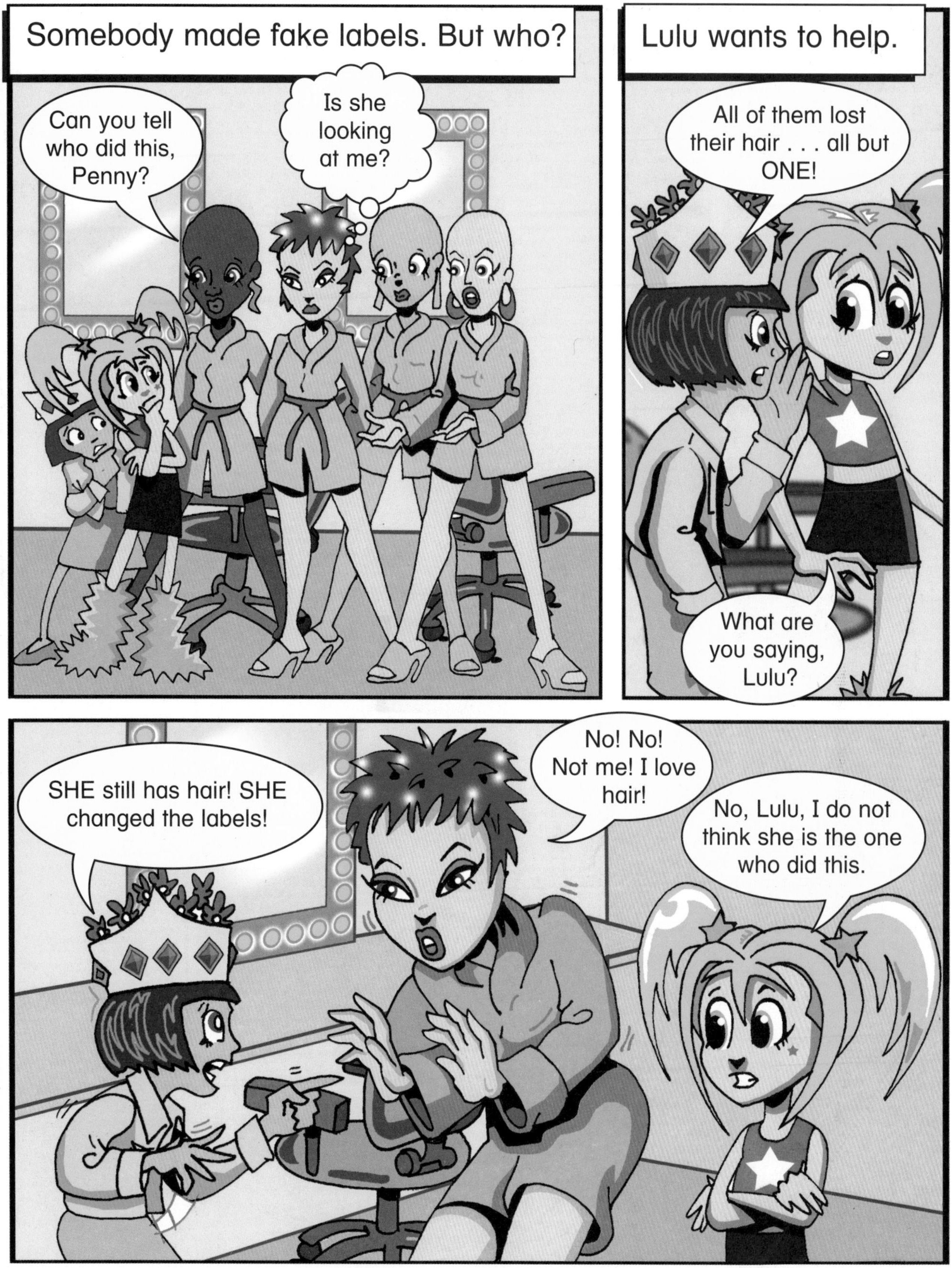
Somebody made fake labels. But who?
Can you tell who did this, Penny?
Is she looking at me?
Lulu wants to help.
All of them lost their hair . . . all but ONE!
What are you saying, Lulu?
SHE still has hair! SHE changed the labels!
No! No! Not me! I love hair!
No, Lulu, I do not think she is the one who did this.

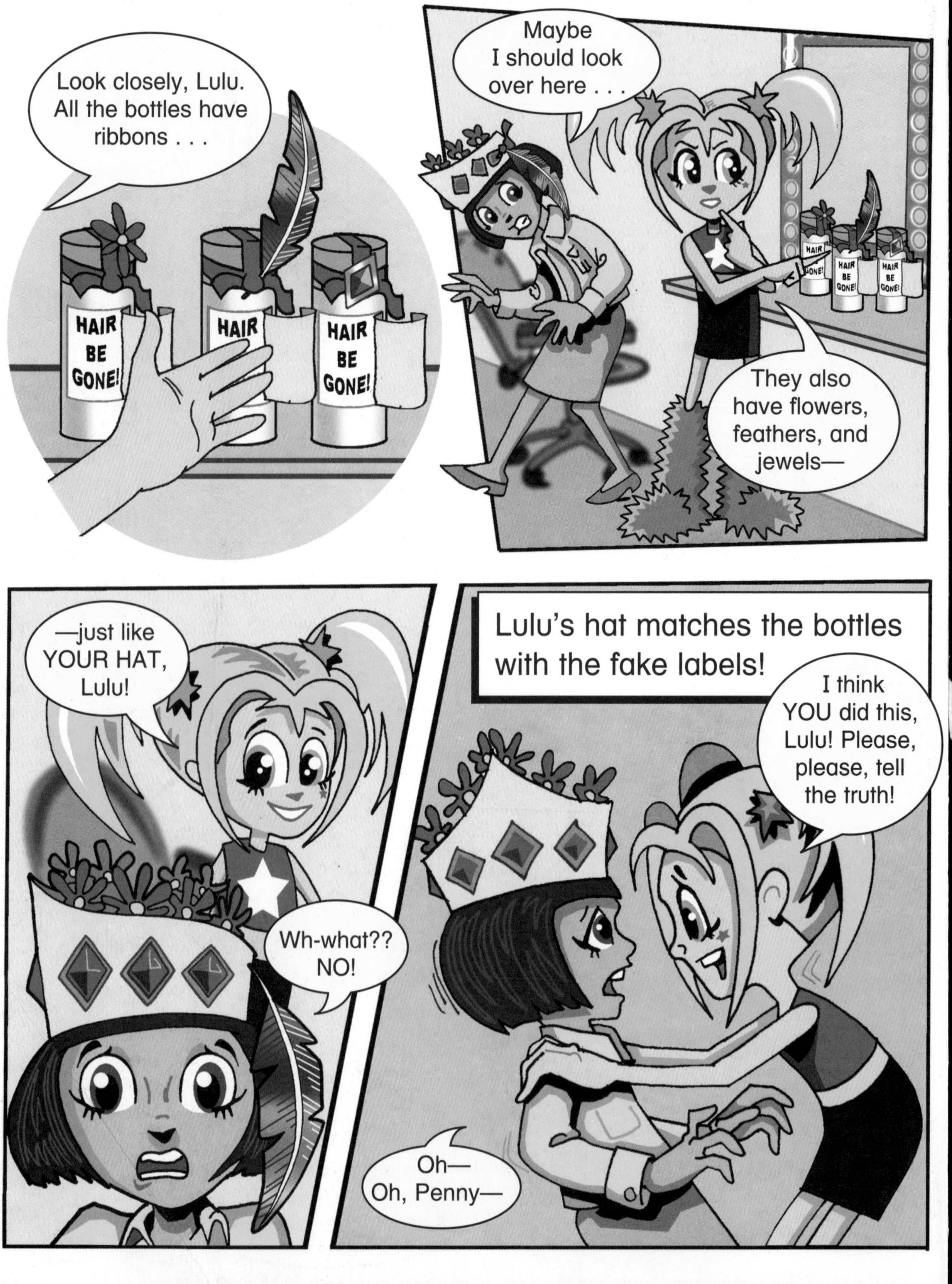
Look closely, Lulu. All the bottles have ribbons . . .
HAIR BE GONE!
HAIR
HAIR BE GONE!
Maybe I should look over here . . .
HAIR BE GONE!
They also have flowers, feathers, and jewels—
—just like YOUR HAT, Lulu!
Wh-what?? NO!
Lulu's hat matches the bottles with the fake labels!
I think YOU did this, Lulu! Please, please, tell the truth!
Oh— Oh, Penny—

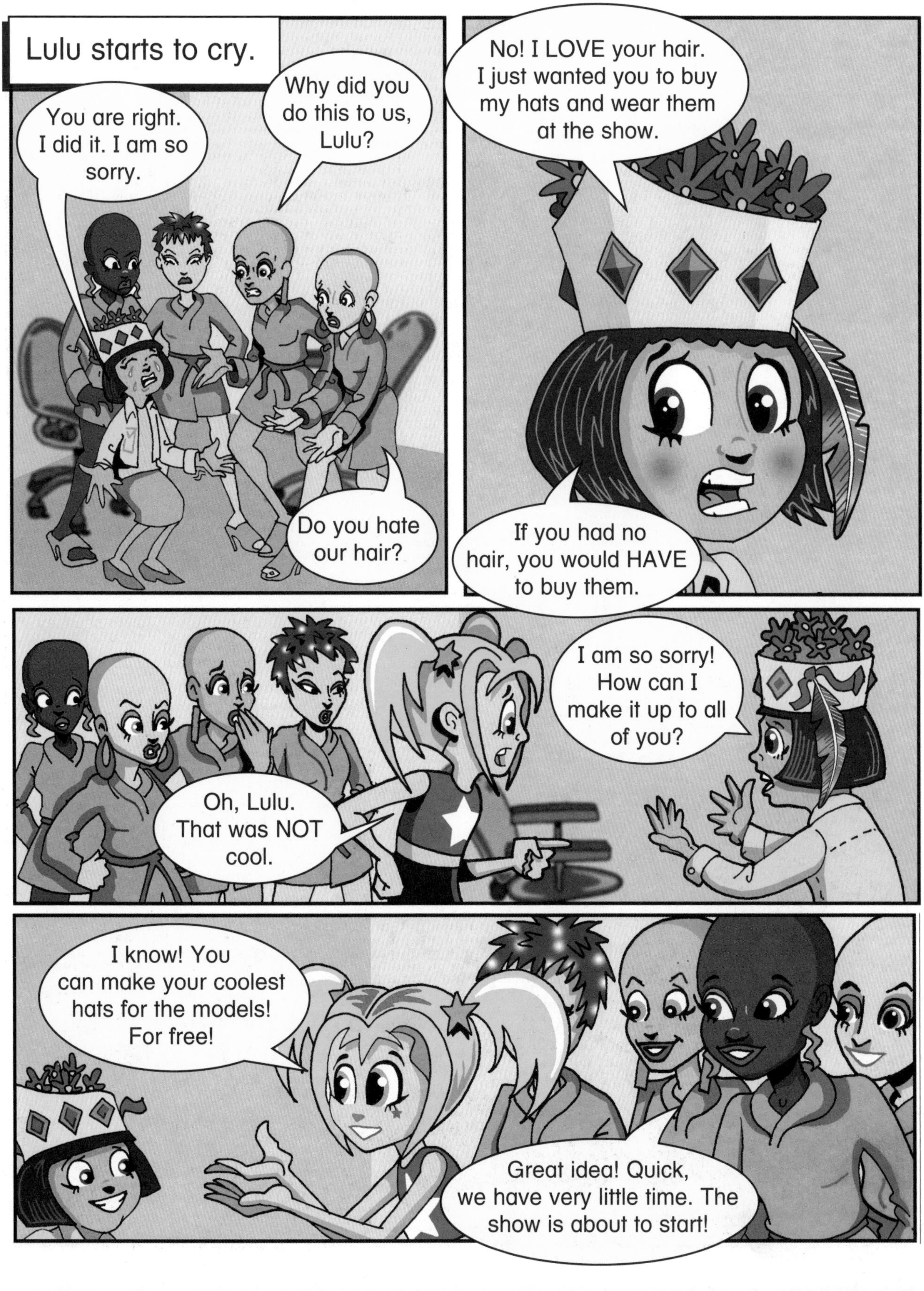
Lulu starts to cry.
Why did you do this to us, Lulu?
You are right. I did it. I am so sorry.
Do you hate our hair?
No! I LOVE your hair. I just wanted you to buy my hats and wear them at the show.
If you had no hair, you would HAVE to buy them.
Oh, Lulu. That was NOT cool.
I am so sorry! How can I make it up to all of you?
I know! You can make your coolest hats for the models! For free!
Great idea! Quick, we have very little time. The show is about to start!

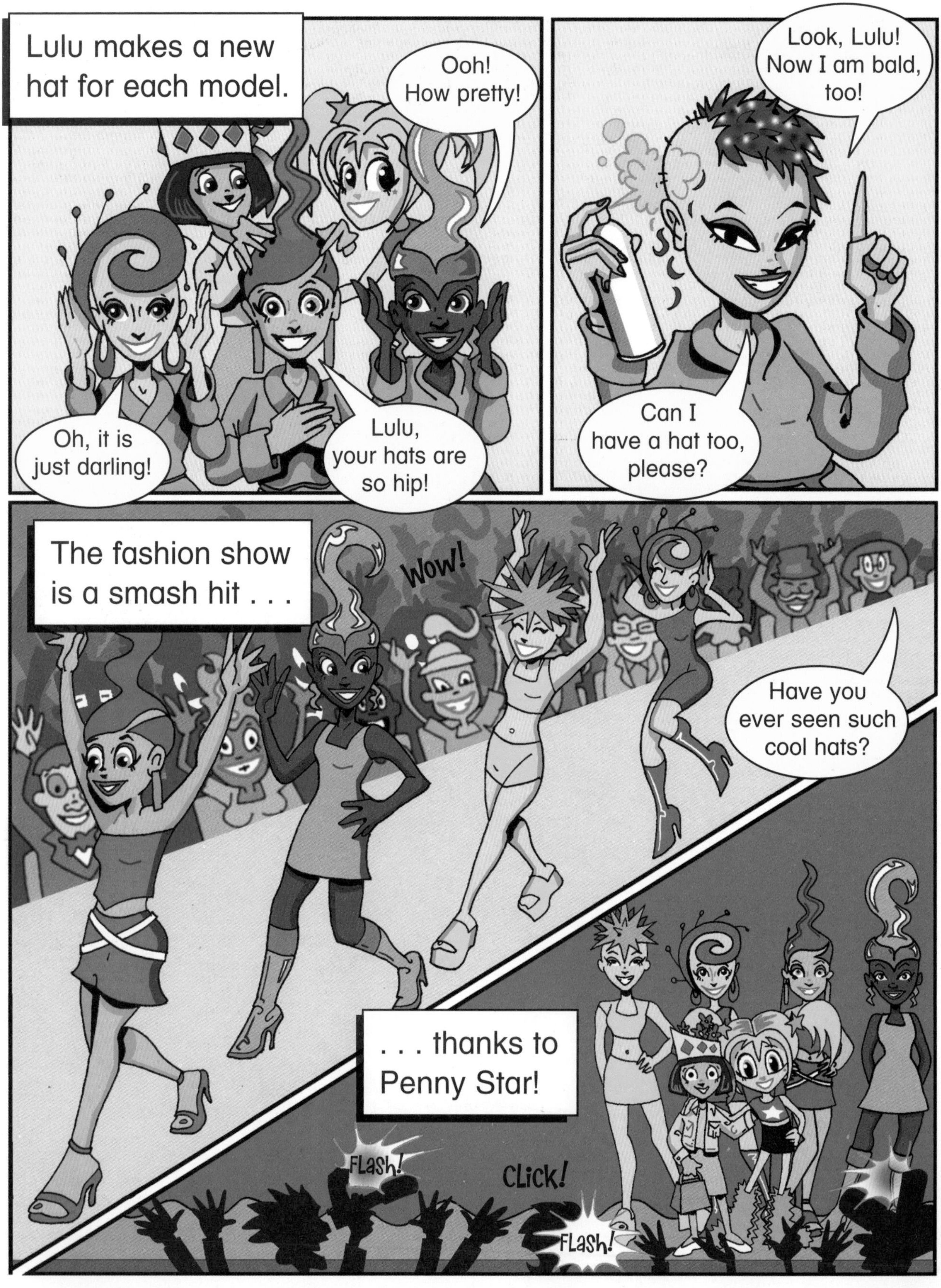

Lulu makes a new hat for each model.
Ooh! How pretty!
Oh, it is just darling!
Lulu, your hats are so hip!
Look, Lulu! Now I am bald, too!
Can I have a hat too, please?
The fashion show is a smash hit . . .
Wow!
Have you ever seen such cool hats?
. . . thanks to Penny Star!
Flash!
Click!
Flash!

TWO OF A KIND

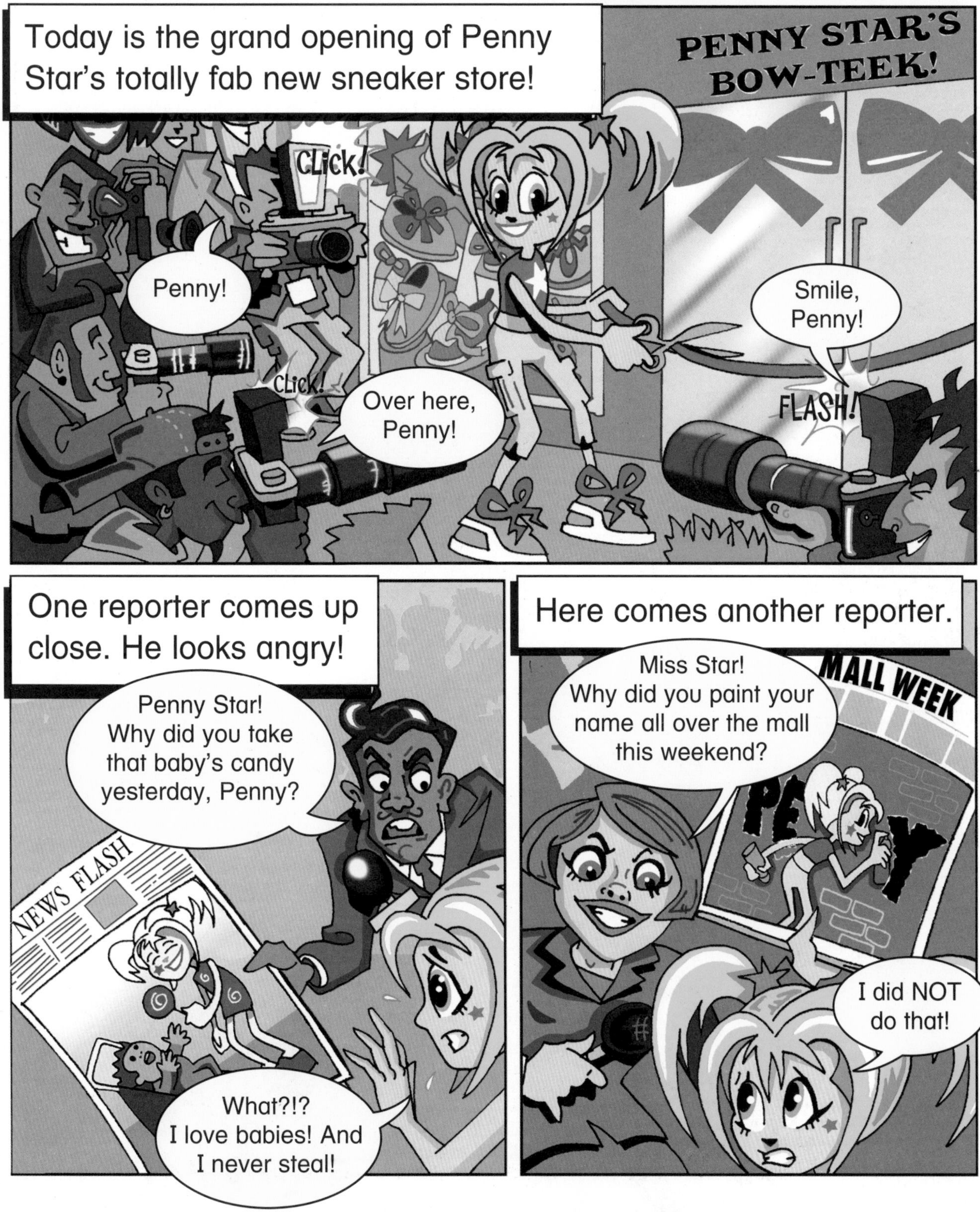

Today is the grand opening of Penny Star's totally fab new sneaker store!
PENNY STAR'S BOW-TEEK!
CLICK!
Penny!
CLICK!
Over here, Penny!
Smile, Penny!
FLASH!
One reporter comes up close. He looks angry!
Penny Star! Why did you take that baby's candy yesterday, Penny?
NEWS FLASH
What?!? I love babies! And I never steal!
Here comes another reporter.
MALL WEEK
Miss Star! Why did you paint your name all over the mall this weekend?
I did NOT do that!

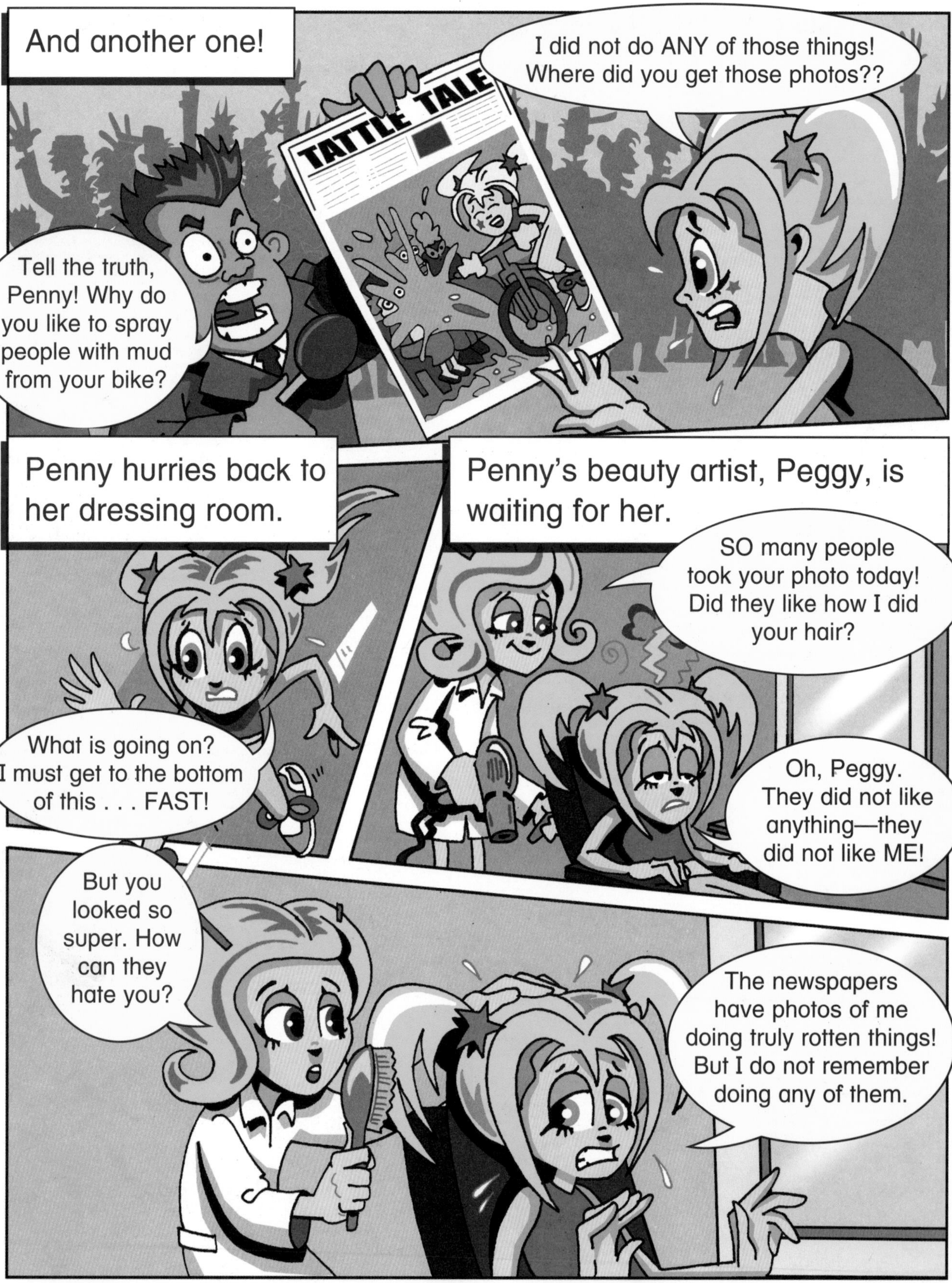

And another one!
TATTLE TALE
I did not do ANY of those things! Where did you get those photos??
Tell the truth, Penny! Why do you like to spray people with mud from your bike?
Penny hurries back to her dressing room.
What is going on? I must get to the bottom of this . . . FAST!
Penny's beauty artist, Peggy, is waiting for her.
SO many people took your photo today! Did they like how I did your hair?
Oh, Peggy. They did not like anything—they did not like ME!
But you looked so super. How can they hate you?
The newspapers have photos of me doing truly rotten things! But I do not remember doing any of them.

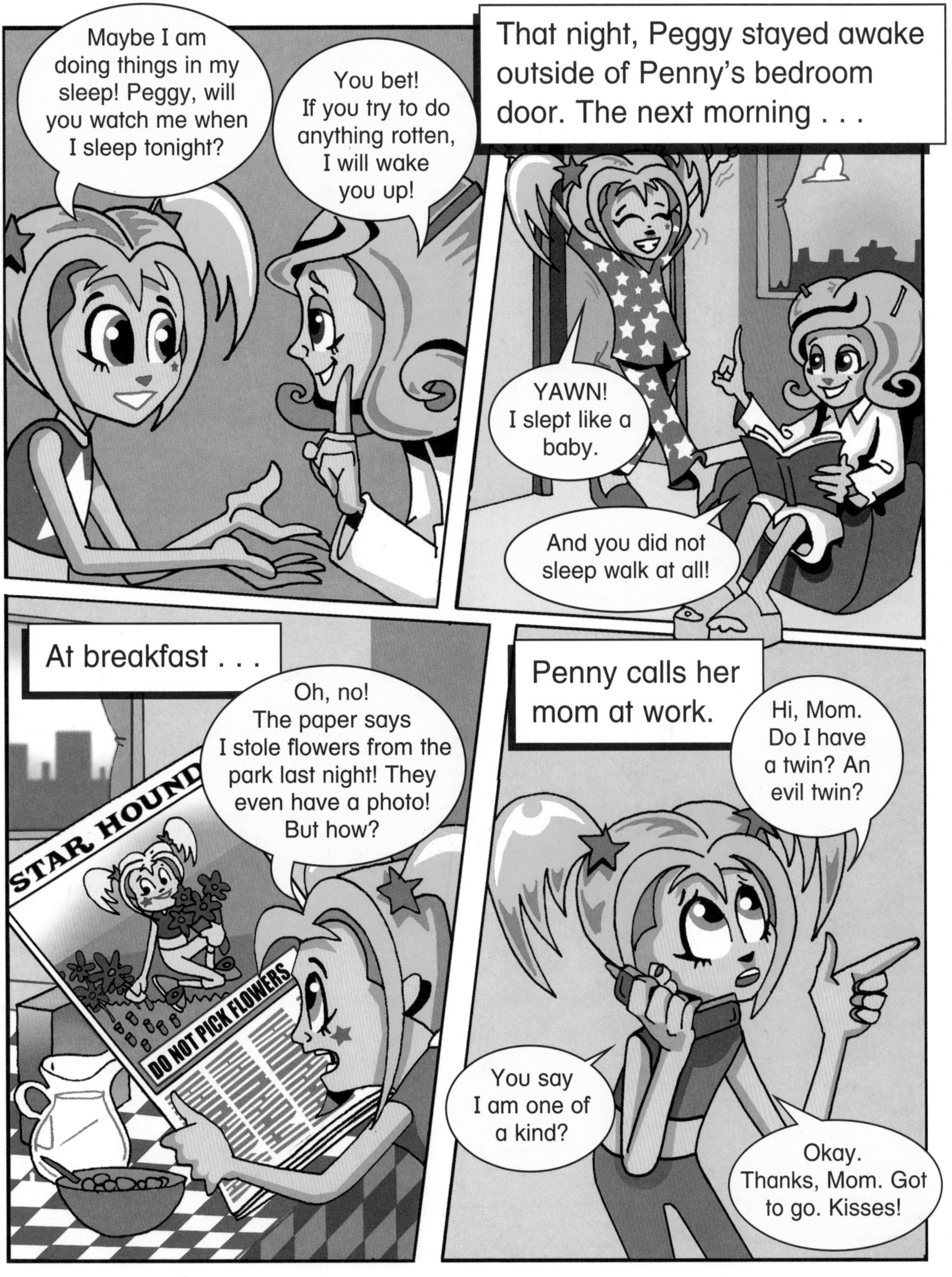
Maybe I am doing things in my sleep! Peggy, will you watch me when I sleep tonight?
You bet! If you try to do anything rotten, I will wake you up!
That night, Peggy stayed awake outside of Penny's bedroom door. The next morning . . .
YAWN! I slept like a baby.
And you did not sleep walk at all!
At breakfast . . .
Oh, no! The paper says I stole flowers from the park last night! They even have a photo! But how?
STAR HOUND
DO NOT PICK FLOWERS
Penny calls her mom at work.
Hi, Mom. Do I have a twin? An evil twin?
You say I am one of a kind?
Okay. Thanks, Mom. Got to go. Kisses!

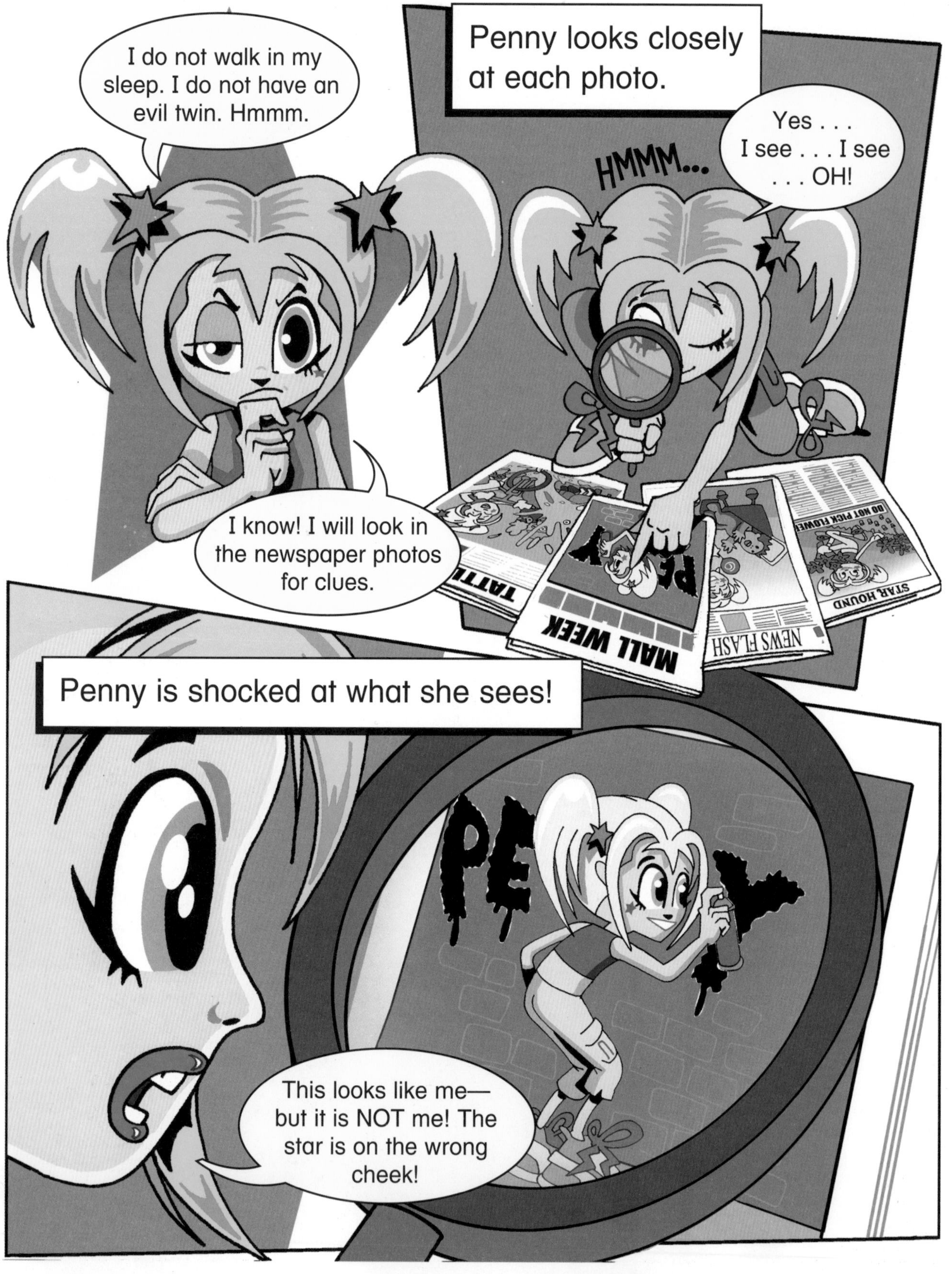
I do not walk in my sleep. I do not have an evil twin. Hmmm.
I know! I will look in the newspaper photos for clues.
Penny looks closely at each photo.
HMMM...
Yes . . . I see . . . I see . . . OH!
MALL WEEK
NEWS FLASH
STAR HOUND
Penny is shocked at what she sees!
This looks like me—but it is NOT me! The star is on the wrong cheek!

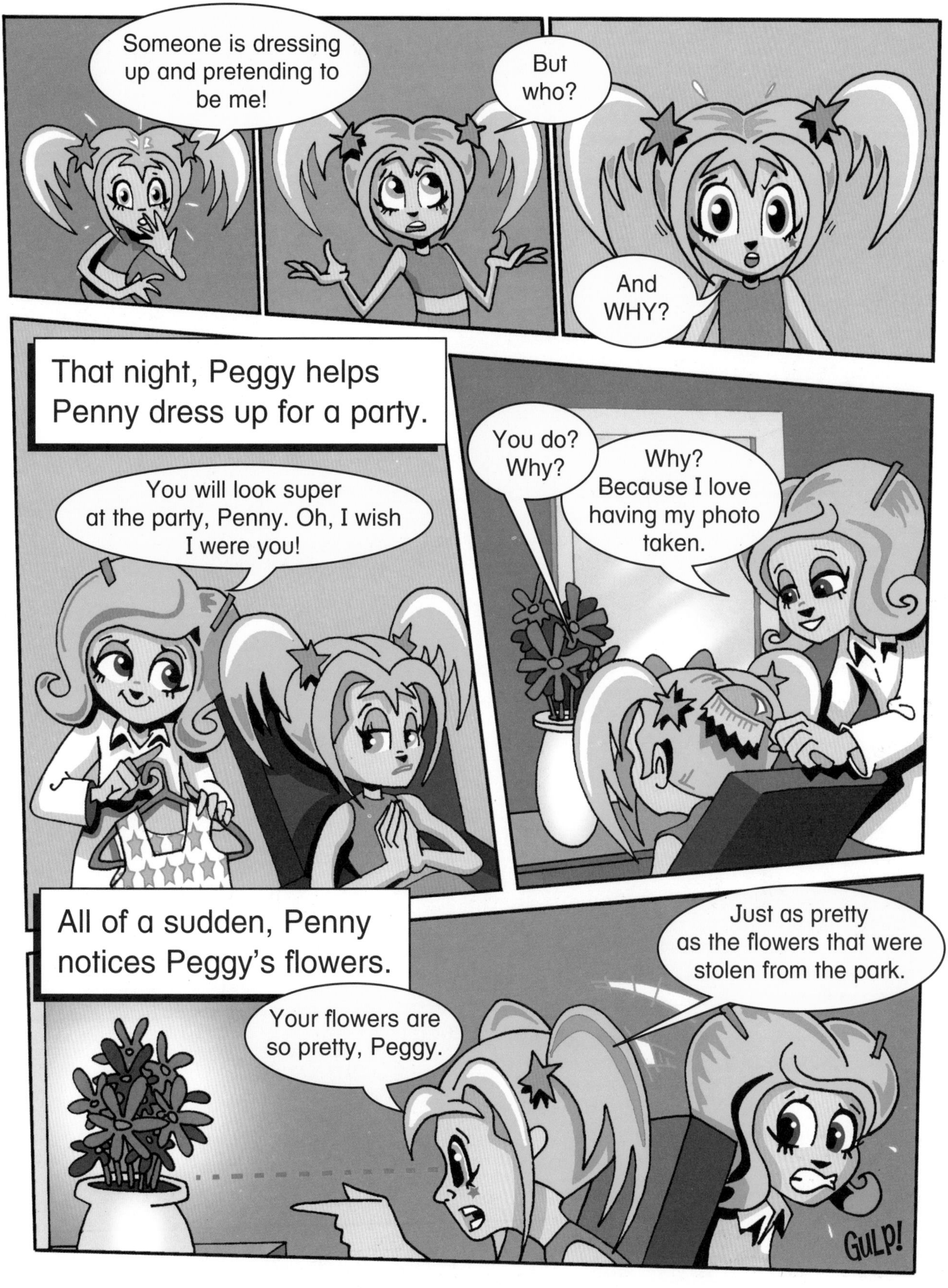

Someone is dressing up and pretending to be me!
But who?
And WHY?
That night, Peggy helps Penny dress up for a party.
You will look super at the party, Penny. Oh, I wish I were you!
You do? Why?
Why? Because I love having my photo taken.
All of a sudden, Penny notices Peggy's flowers.
Your flowers are so pretty, Peggy.
Just as pretty as the flowers that were stolen from the park.
GULP!

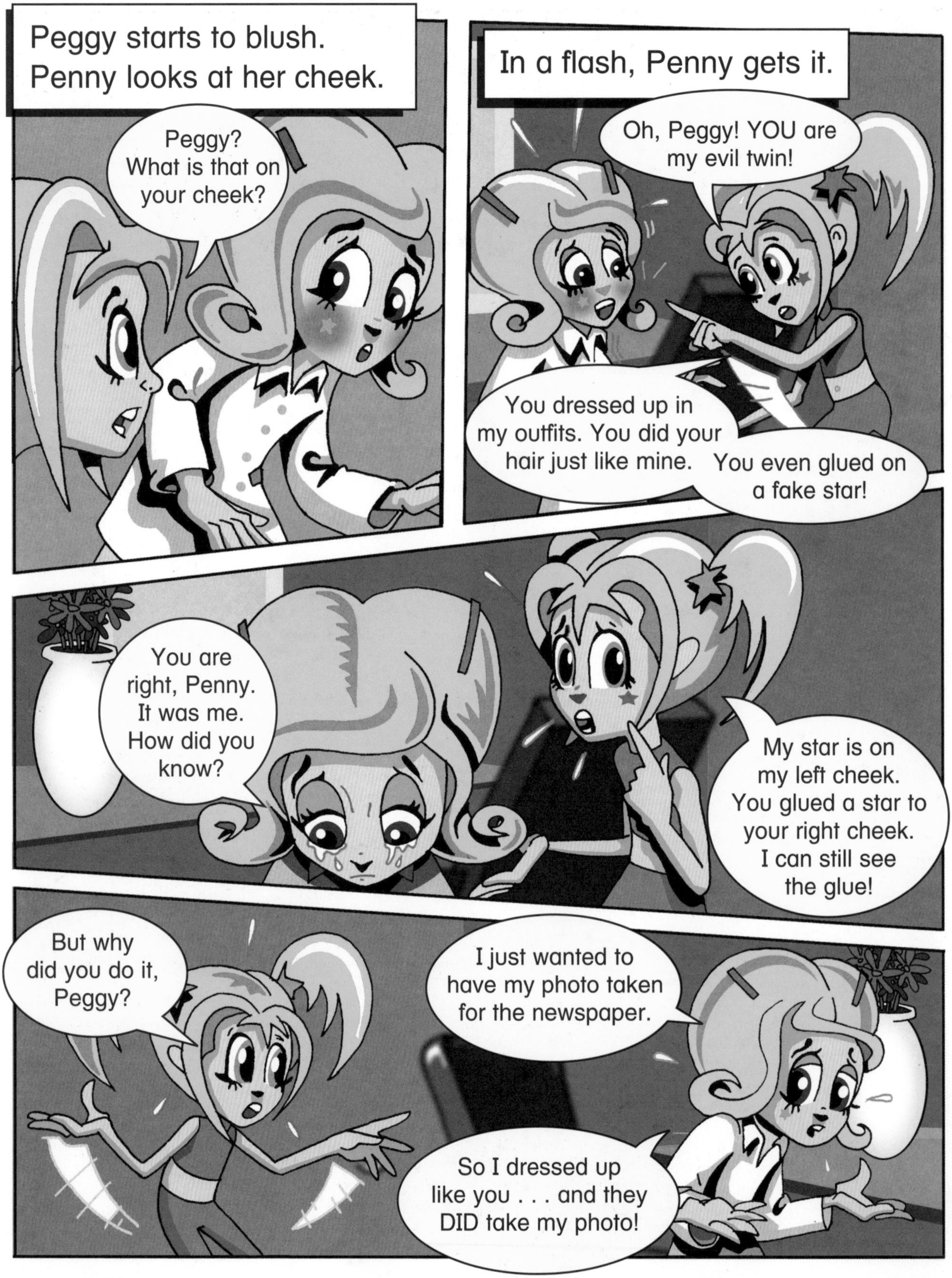
Peggy starts to blush. Penny looks at her cheek.
Peggy? What is that on your cheek?
In a flash, Penny gets it.
Oh, Peggy! YOU are my evil twin!
You dressed up in my outfits. You did your hair just like mine.
You even glued on a fake star!
You are right, Penny. It was me. How did you know?
My star is on my left cheek. You glued a star to your right cheek. I can still see the glue!
But why did you do it, Peggy?
I just wanted to have my photo taken for the newspaper.
So I dressed up like you . . . and they DID take my photo!

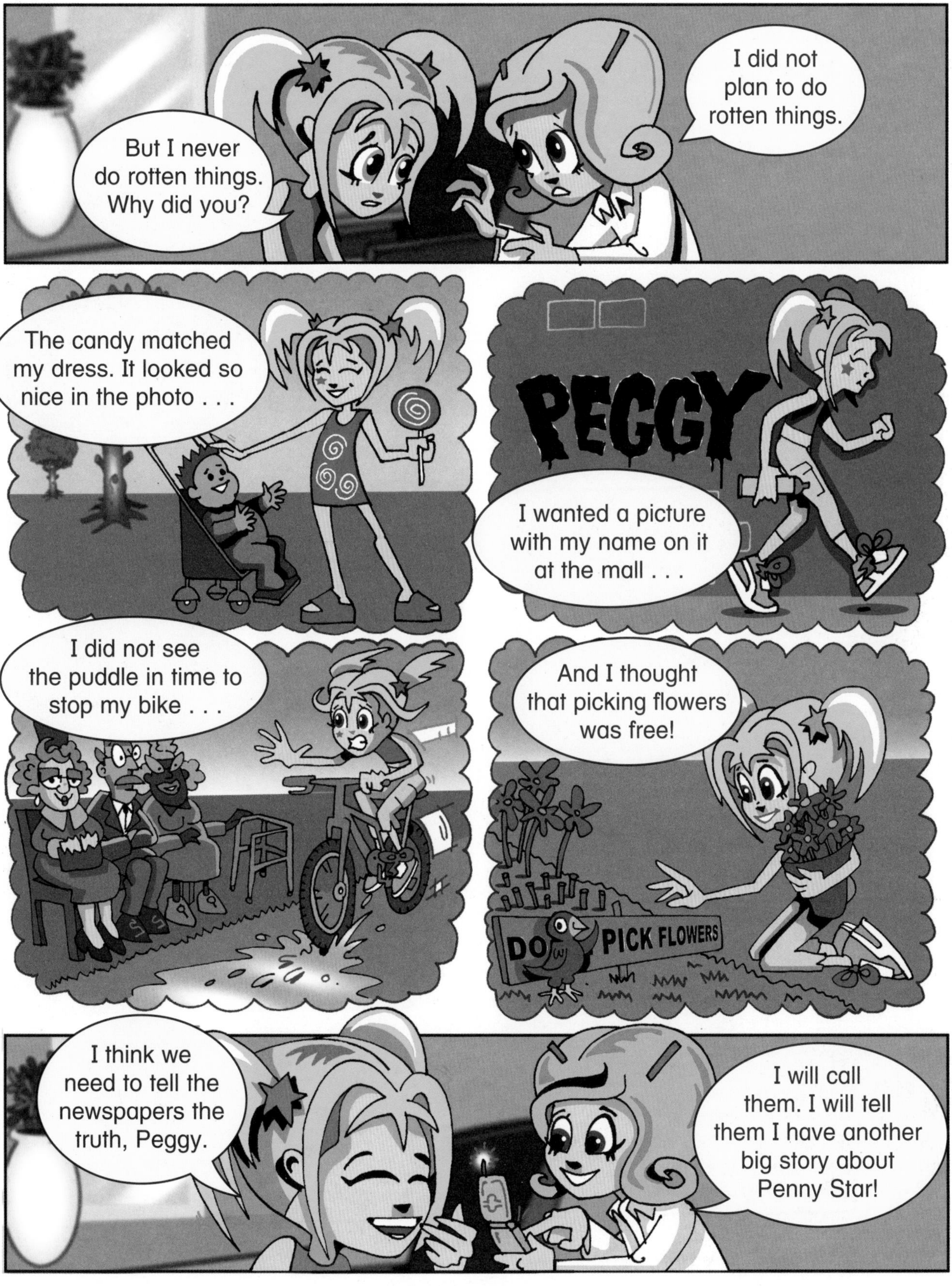
But I never do rotten things. Why did you?
I did not plan to do rotten things.
The candy matched my dress. It looked so nice in the photo . . .
PEGGY
I wanted a picture with my name on it at the mall . . .
I did not see the puddle in time to stop my bike . . .
And I thought that picking flowers was free!
DO PICK FLOWERS
I think we need to tell the newspapers the truth, Peggy.
I will call them. I will tell them I have another big story about Penny Star!

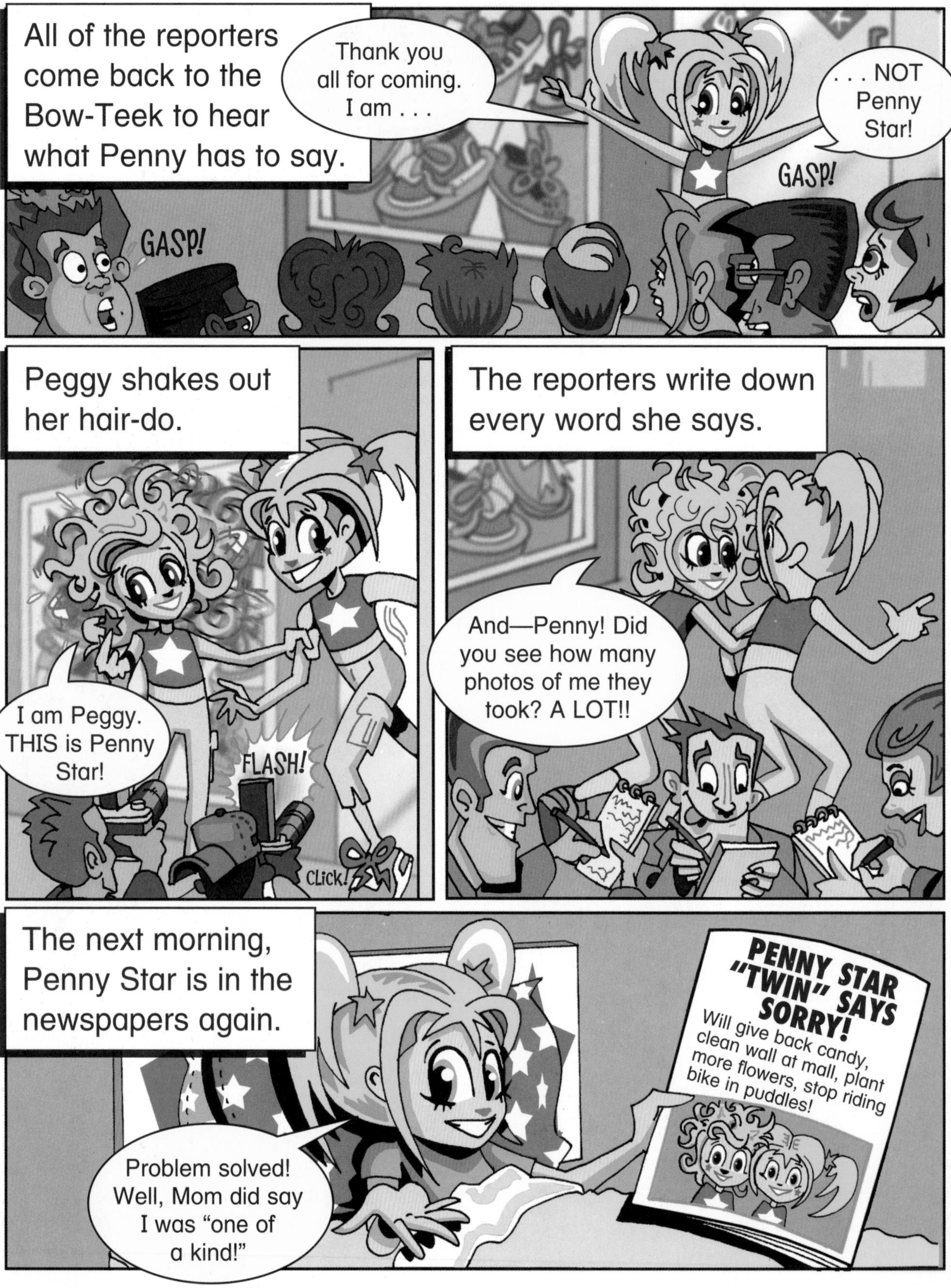
All of the reporters come back to the Bow-Teek to hear what Penny has to say.
Thank you all for coming. I am . . .
. . . NOT Penny Star!
GASP!
GASP!
Peggy shakes out her hair-do.
I am Peggy. THIS is Penny Star!
FLASH!
CLICK!
The reporters write down every word she says.
And—Penny! Did you see how many photos of me they took? A LOT!!
The next morning, Penny Star is in the newspapers again.
PENNY STAR "TWIN" SAYS SORRY!
Will give back candy, clean wall at mall, plant more flowers, stop riding bike in puddles!
Problem solved! Well, Mom did say I was "one of a kind!"

SCRATCH FASHION

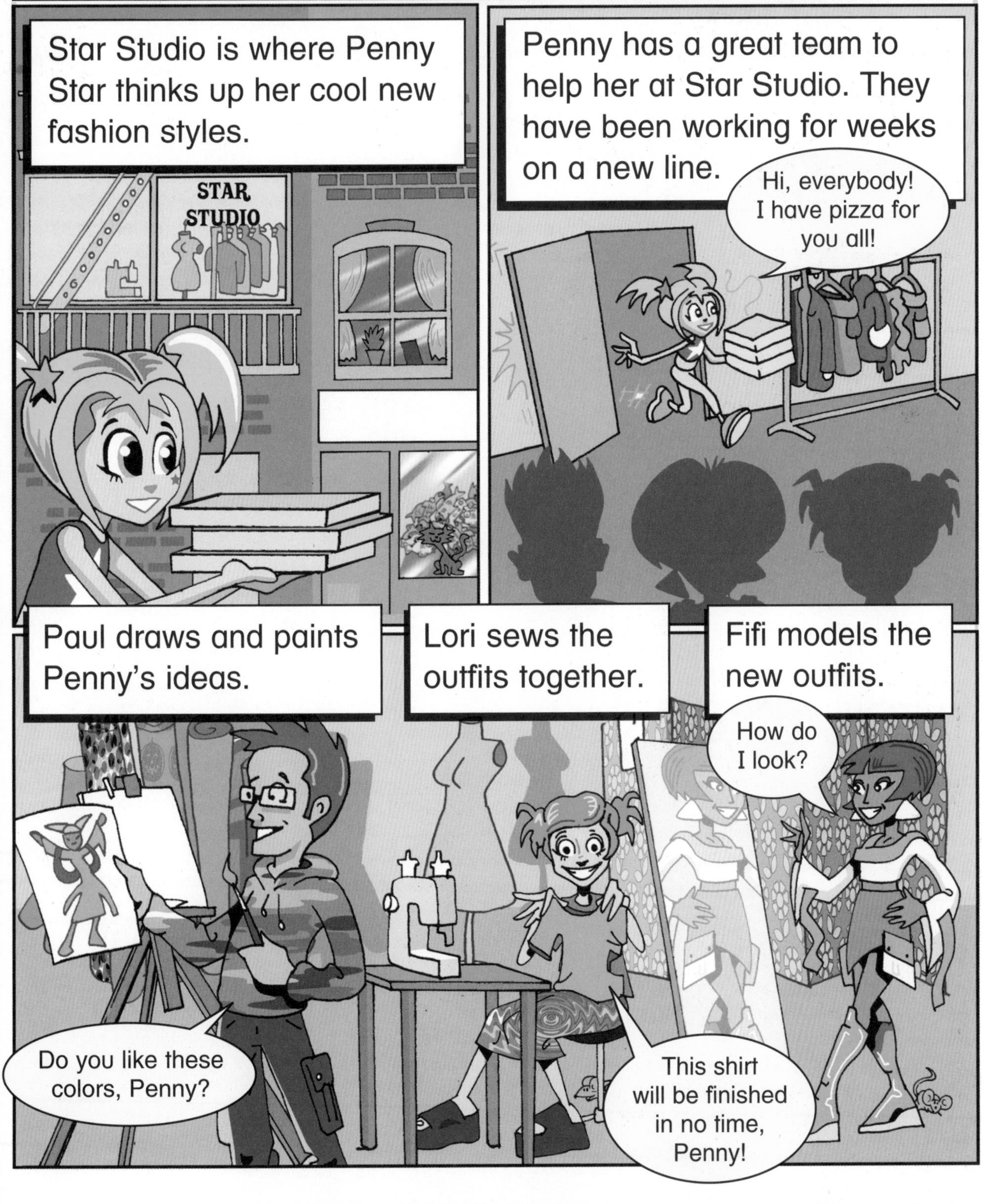
Star Studio is where Penny Star thinks up her cool new fashion styles.
STAR STUDIO
Penny has a great team to help her at Star Studio. They have been working for weeks on a new line.
Hi, everybody! I have pizza for you all!
Paul draws and paints Penny's ideas.
Lori sews the outfits together.
Fifi models the new outfits.
How do I look?
Do you like these colors, Penny?
This shirt will be finished in no time, Penny!

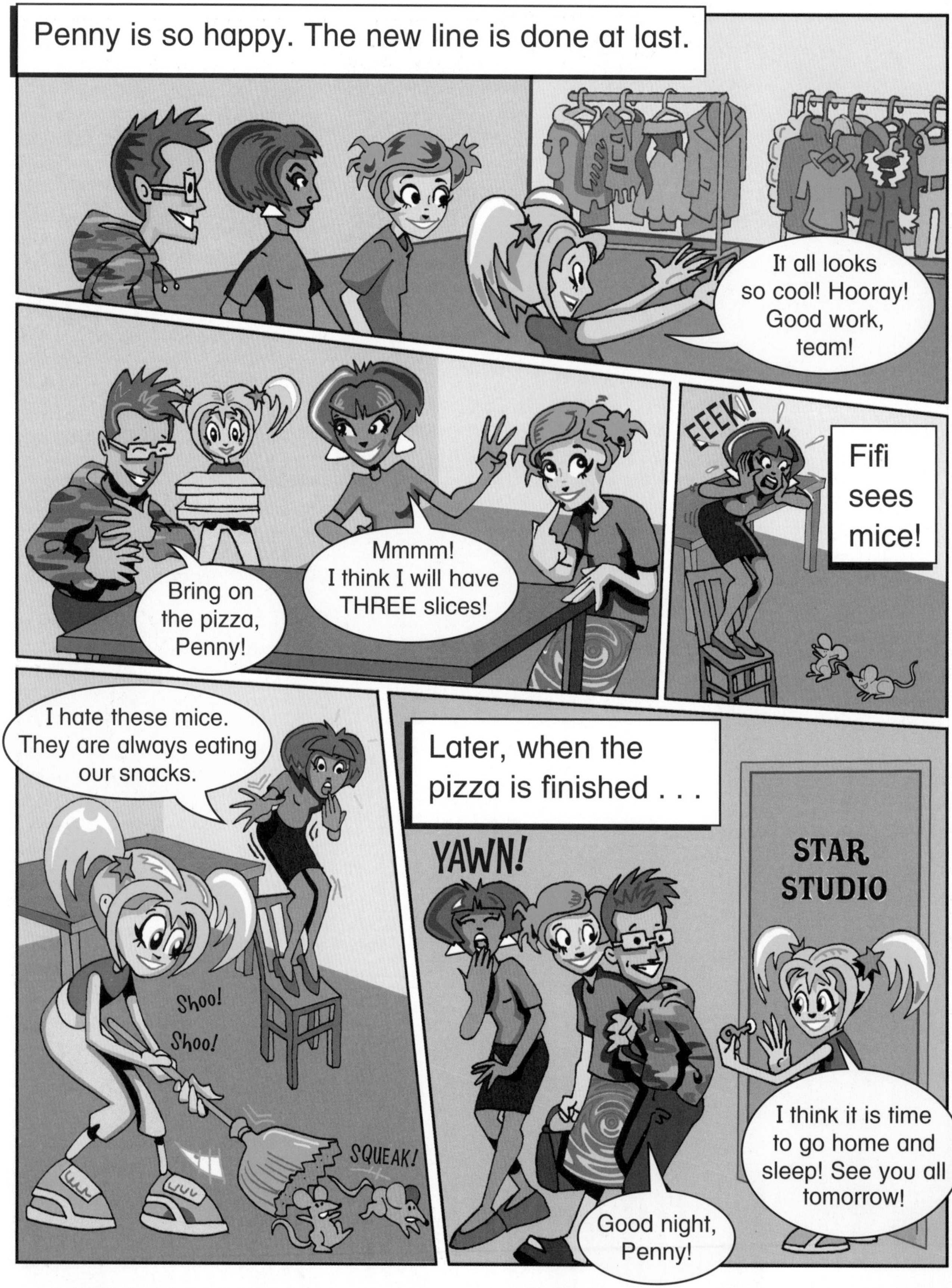
Penny is so happy. The new line is done at last.
It all looks so cool! Hooray! Good work, team!
Bring on the pizza, Penny!
Mmmm! I think I will have THREE slices!
EEEK!
Fifi sees mice!
I hate these mice. They are always eating our snacks.
Shoo!
Shoo!
SQUEAK!
Later, when the pizza is finished . . .
YAWN!
STAR STUDIO
I think it is time to go home and sleep! See you all tomorrow!
Good night, Penny!

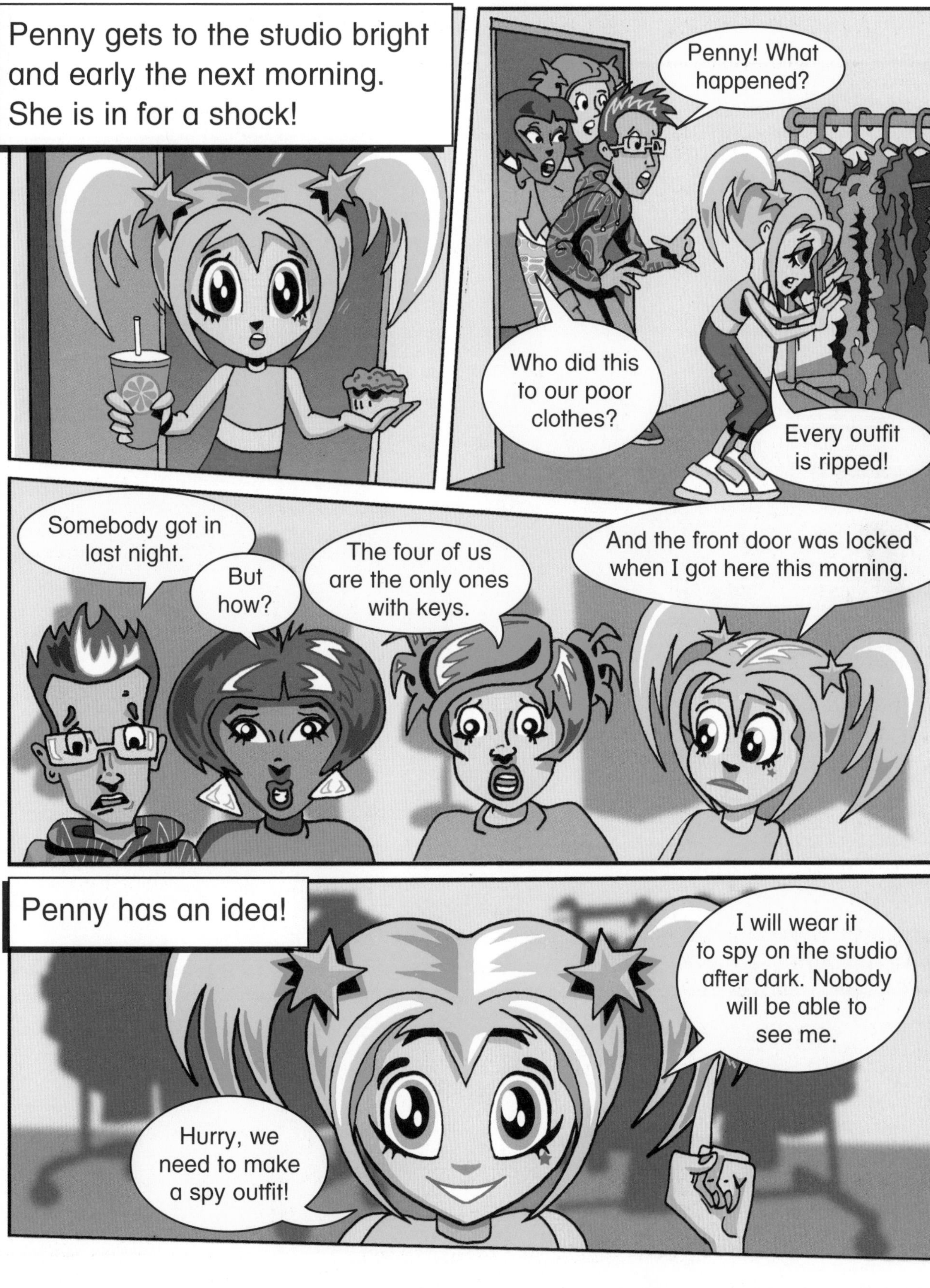
Penny gets to the studio bright and early the next morning. She is in for a shock!
Penny! What happened?
Who did this to our poor clothes?
Every outfit is ripped!
Somebody got in last night.
But how?
The four of us are the only ones with keys.
And the front door was locked when I got here this morning.
Penny has an idea!
Hurry, we need to make a spy outfit!
I will wear it to spy on the studio after dark. Nobody will be able to see me.

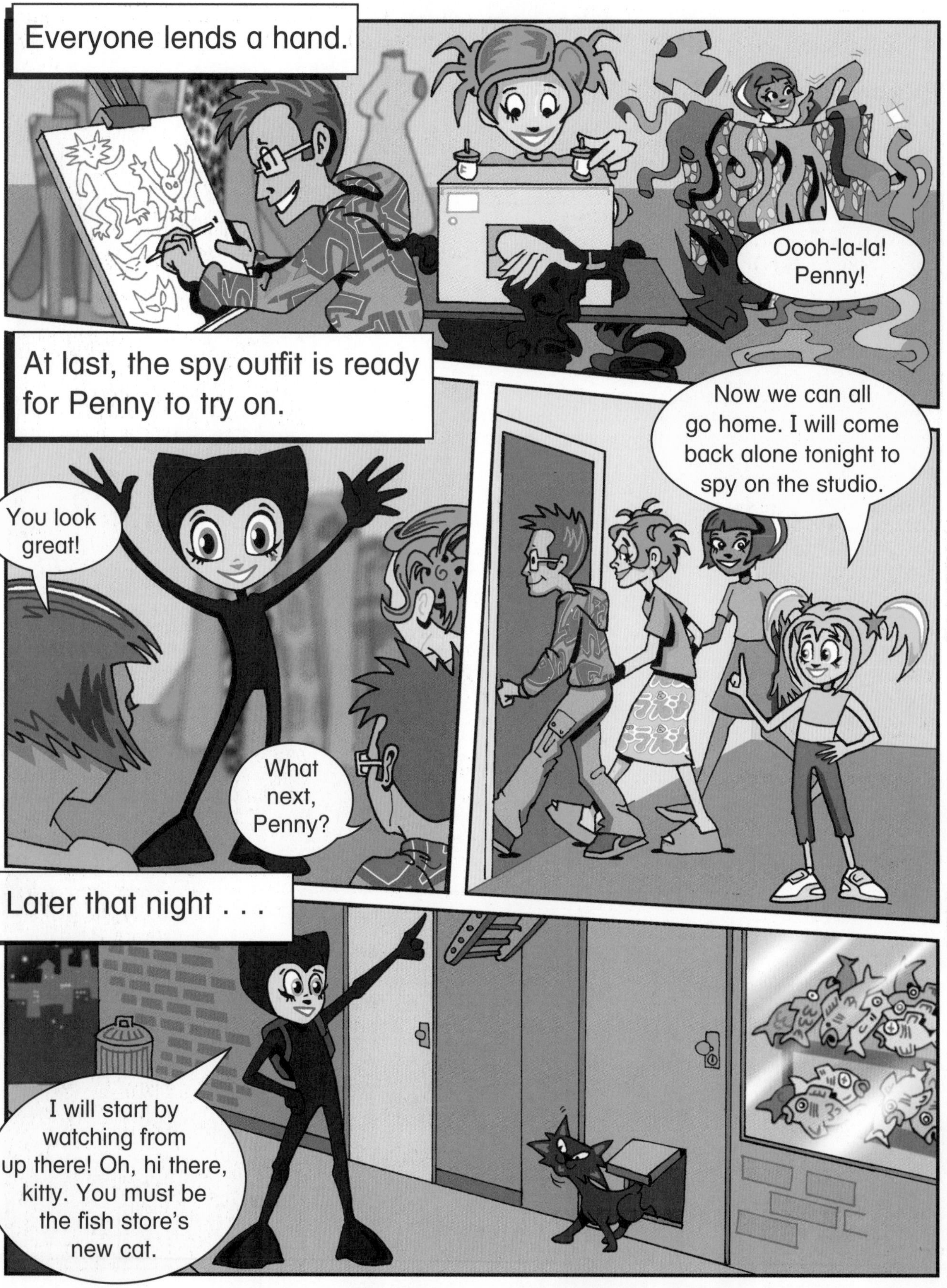
Everyone lends a hand.
Oooh-la-la! Penny!
At last, the spy outfit is ready for Penny to try on.
You look great!
What next, Penny?
Now we can all go home. I will come back alone tonight to spy on the studio.
Later that night . . .
I will start by watching from up there! Oh, hi there, kitty. You must be the fish store's new cat.

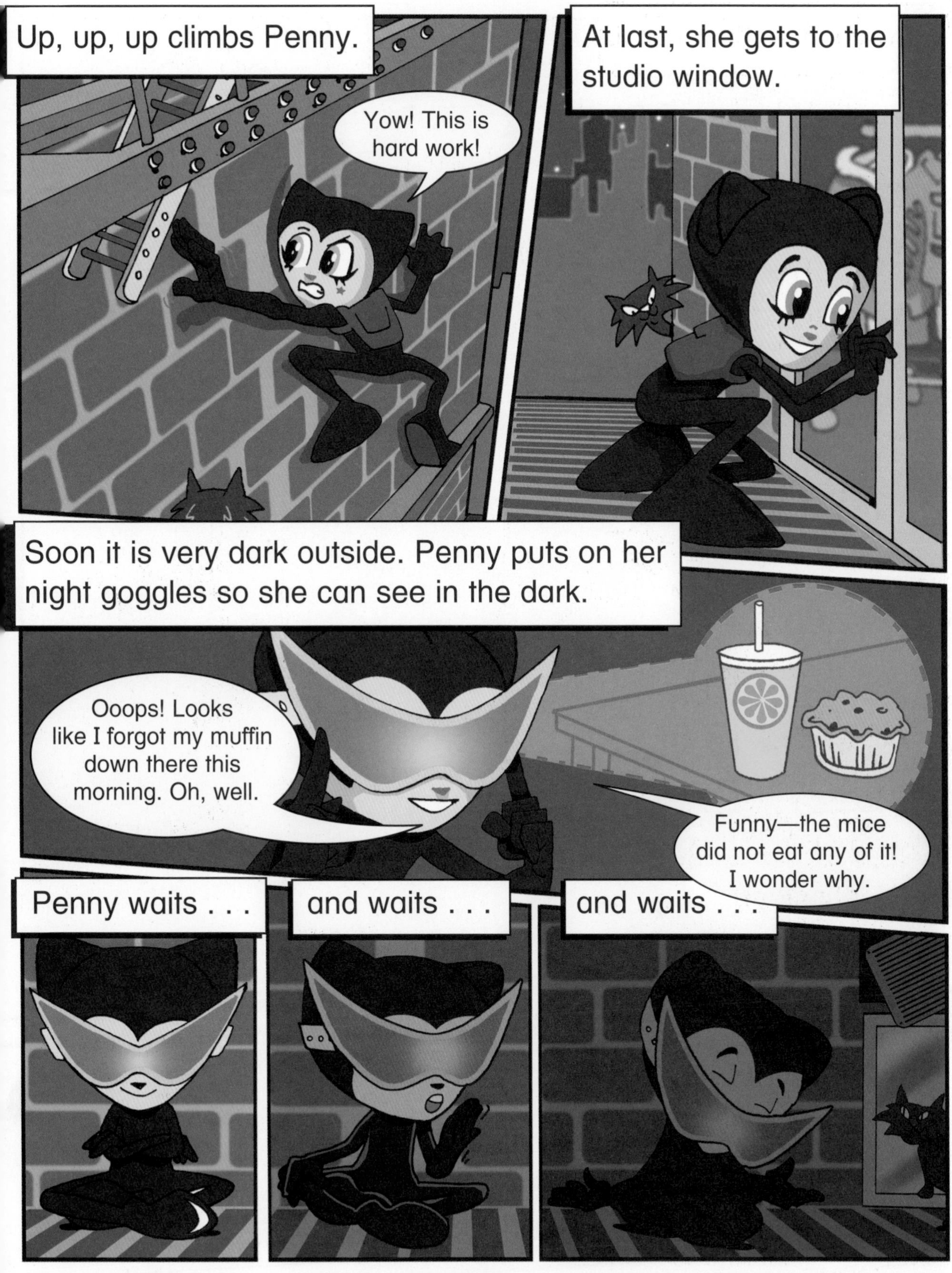
Up, up, up climbs Penny.
Yow! This is hard work!
At last, she gets to the studio window.
Soon it is very dark outside. Penny puts on her night goggles so she can see in the dark.
Ooops! Looks like I forgot my muffin down there this morning. Oh, well.
Funny—the mice did not eat any of it! I wonder why.
Penny waits . . .
and waits . . .
and waits . . .

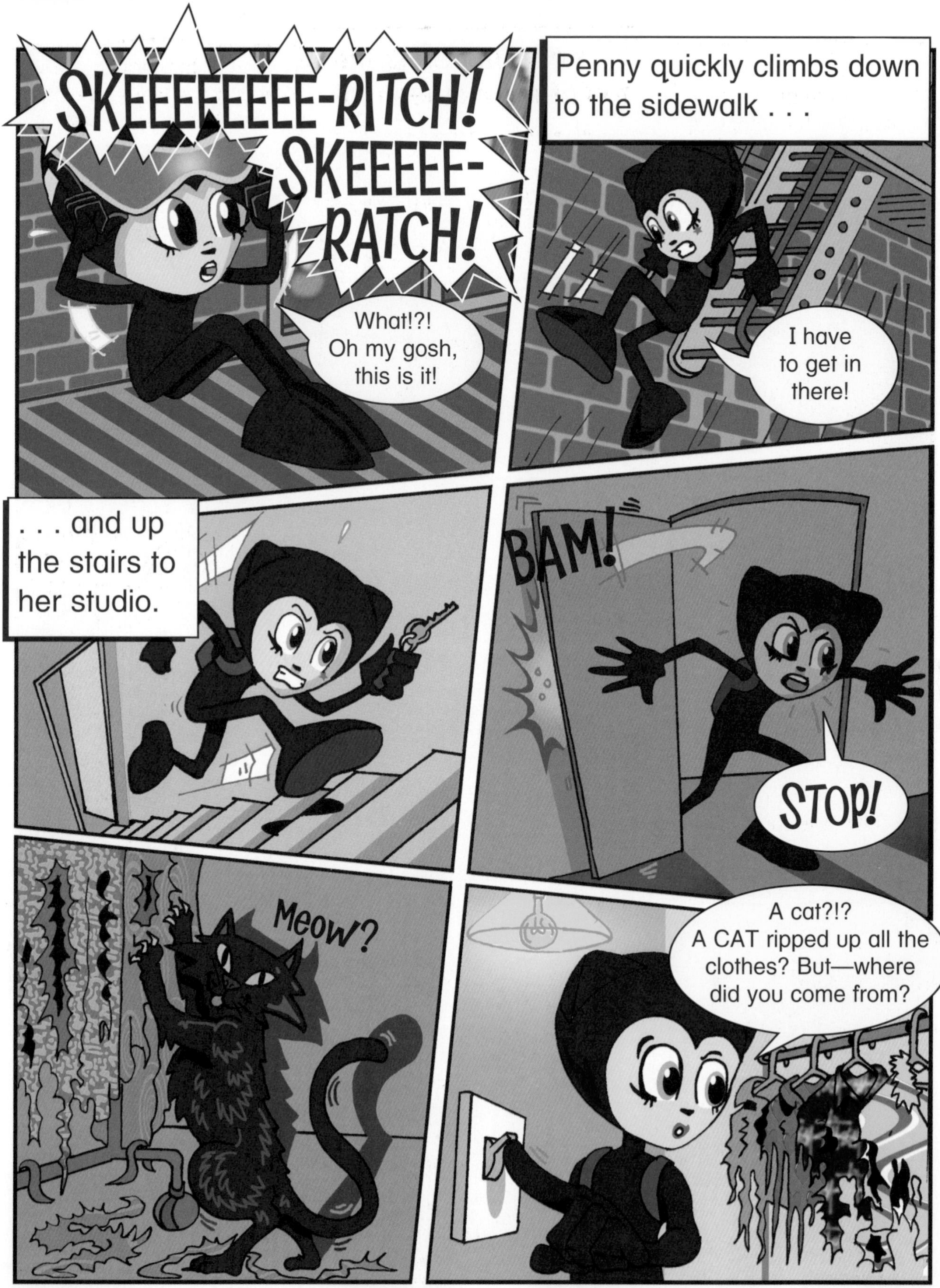
SKEEEEEEEE-RITCH! SKEEEEE-RATCH!
What!?! Oh my gosh, this is it!
Penny quickly climbs down to the sidewalk . . .
I have to get in there!
. . . and up the stairs to her studio.
BAM!
STOP!
Meow?
A cat?!? A CAT ripped up all the clothes? But—where did you come from?

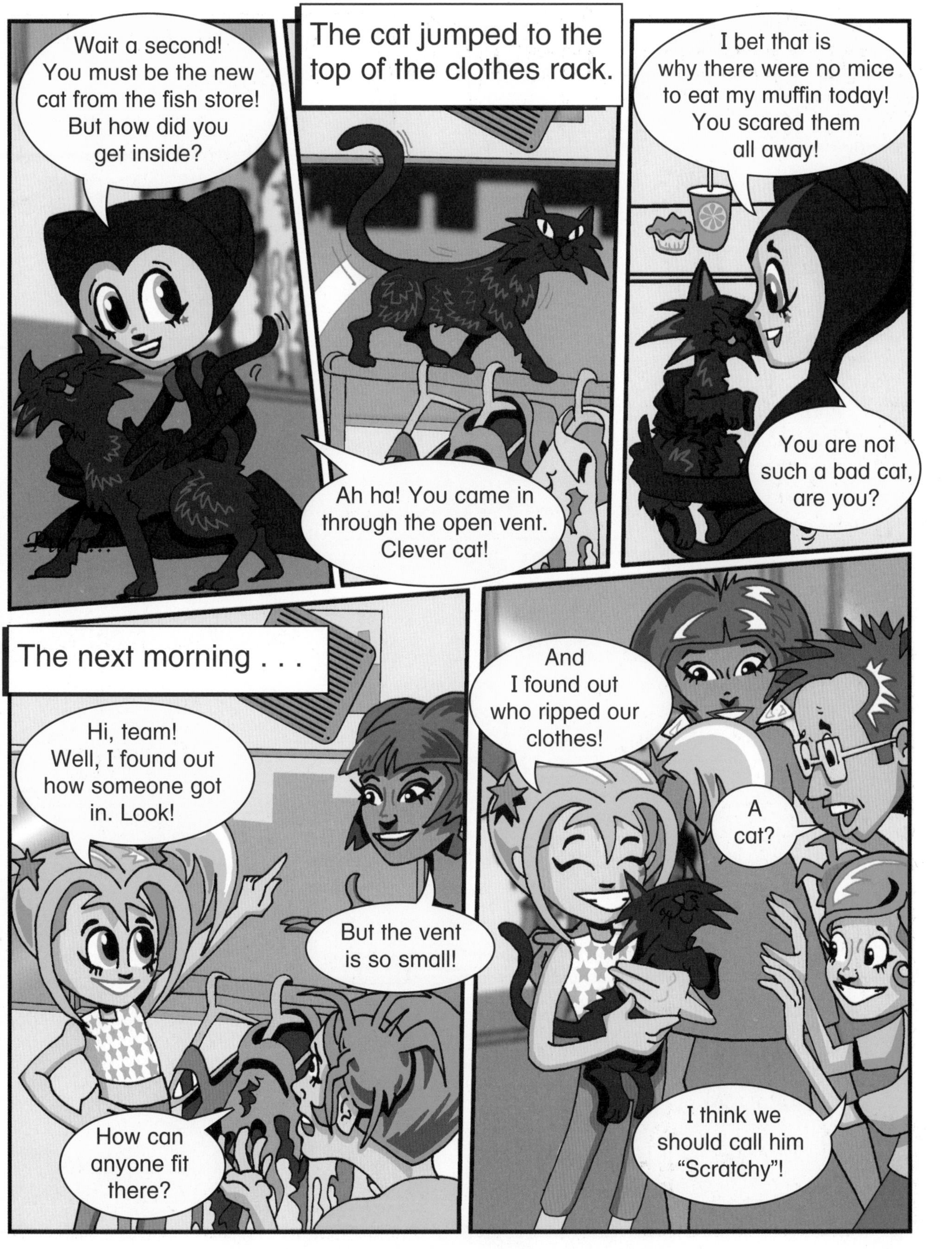
Wait a second! You must be the new cat from the fish store! But how did you get inside?
The cat jumped to the top of the clothes rack.
Ah ha! You came in through the open vent. Clever cat!
I bet that is why there were no mice to eat my muffin today! You scared them all away!
You are not such a bad cat, are you?
The next morning . . .
Hi, team! Well, I found out how someone got in. Look!
But the vent is so small!
How can anyone fit there?
And I found out who ripped our clothes!
A cat?
I think we should call him "Scratchy"!

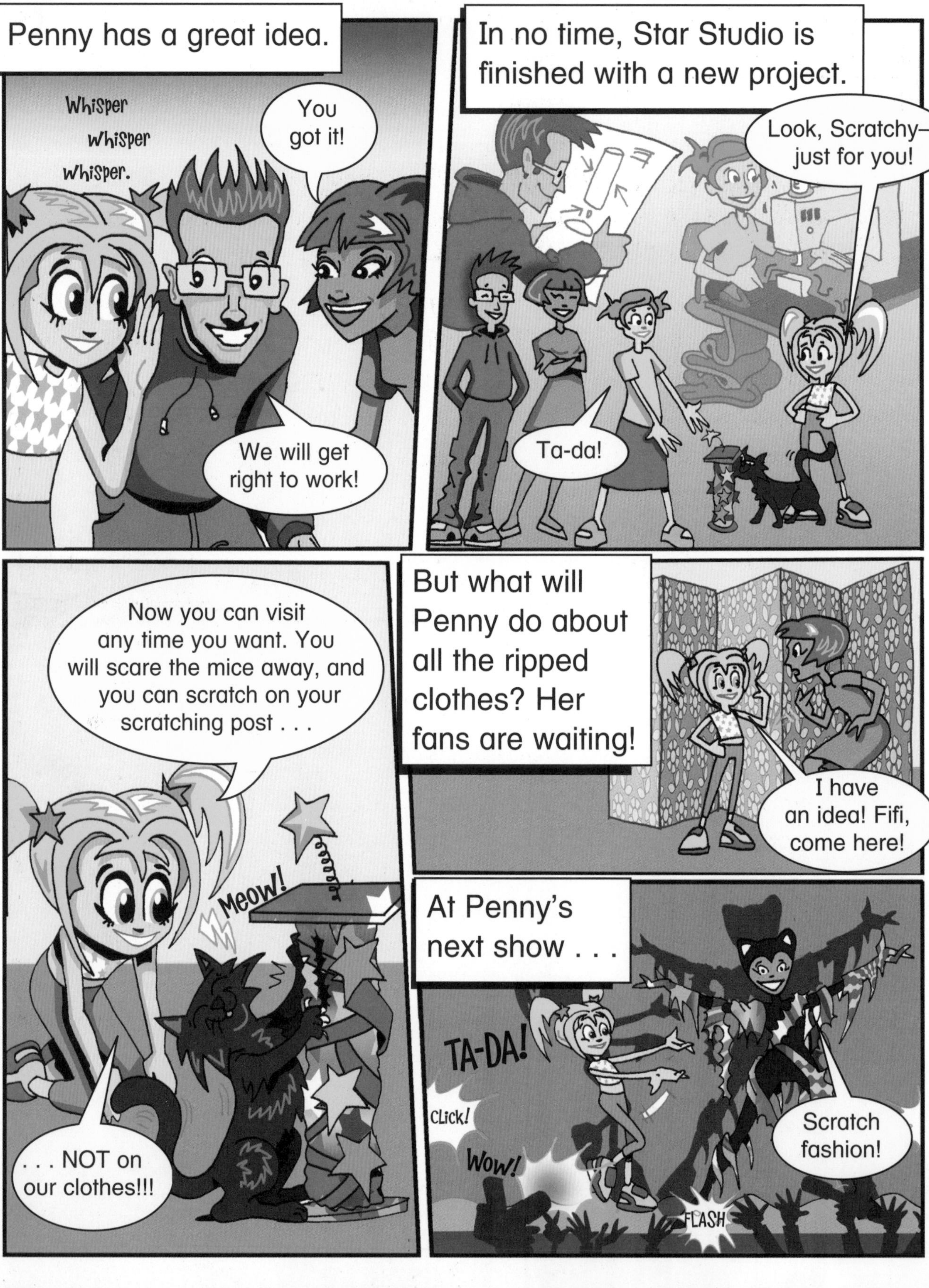
Penny has a great idea.
Whisper whisper whisper.
You got it!
We will get right to work!
In no time, Star Studio is finished with a new project.
Look, Scratchy— just for you!
Ta-da!
Now you can visit any time you want. You will scare the mice away, and you can scratch on your scratching post . . .
Meow!
. . . NOT on our clothes!!!
But what will Penny do about all the ripped clothes? Her fans are waiting!
I have an idea! Fifi, come here!
At Penny's next show . . .
TA-DA!
Click!
Wow!
FLASH
Scratch fashion!